Lucy and the Sea Monster

Karen Dolby

Illustrated by Caroline Church

Design Consultant: Amanda Barlow
Series Editor: Gaby Waters
Assistant Editor: Michelle Bates

Contents

About this Book

This story is about Lucy and Tom Cat. They are on their way to the beach where their amazing adventure begins.

LUCY

TOM CAT

Keep your eyes open for clues. If you get stuck there are answers on pages 31 and 32.

Turn the page for a great adventure.

On the Beach

Lucy sat on a rock on the beach, reading a fantastic adventure story about dragons and monsters. Tom Cat was nearby watching fish jump.

Waves lapped against Lucy's rock and crashed onto the shore. Her tummy rumbled. It was nearly supper time.

Tom Cat yowled as a wave washed over him. Lucy looked up. She couldn't see anything. But there was something that Lucy had not spotted. It was in the water, coming closer and closer.

Look at the opposite page. Can you see what it is?

Lucy Meets the Sea Monster

Lucy turned around and gulped as the monster reared up out of the waves. She had never seen anything like it before, except in her book. It was green, with a long snaky body, knobbled skin and wobbly antennae on its head. It had spikes like a dragon along its back, but it looked friendly.

Imagine Lucy's surprise when the strange creature began to speak.

"Hello," it said. "My name's Horace. I'm a sea monster."

"H . . . h . . . hello," stammered Lucy. "I'm Lucy and this is Tom Cat." But where WAS Tom Cat? He had vanished.

Can you spot Tom Cat?

The Adventure Begins

"I must rescue Tom Cat!" Lucy exclaimed.

"I'll help you," said Horace. "Climb onto my back."

Lucy looked doubtfully at Horace's spikes, but when she touched one it was surprisingly soft. She jumped up and held on tightly. Horace's tail snaked from side to side and they whizzed away, whooshing through the waves.

A sleek silvery shape suddenly leapt up and dived quickly down again, but not before Lucy caught sight of a beady eye and cheeky, friendly grin.

Dolphins!
There were lots of
them on all sides,
chattering and dancing around
Horace and Lucy.
"Have you seen my cat?" Lucy asked them.
"Try Blue Bird Island," one called, pushing a map
of the islands into Lucy's hand.

Which one do you think is Blue Bird Island?

Blue Bird Island

"We're here," Horace said, cheerily.

Lucy jumped ashore on Blue Bird Island and heard the sounds of splashing and shouting nearby. She raced along the rocky beach and found some children tying up their boat. Lucy was aware of eyes watching in the distance, behind the trees.

There was no sign of Tom Cat here, but one of the children had seen him and the others gave her helpful directions. She had to find One Tree Island. Lucy stared at the islands across the bay.

Can you find One Tree Island?

The island has a tower on it . . .

. . . with a pointed turret, like a witch's hat . . .

. . . and no other buildings.

Finn the Fishergirl

Horace zipped across to One Tree Island where they met a little fishergirl. She began to speak to them, but what she said was in rhyme.

*"Finn is my name
and if you'll help with my game,
I'll put you on track
to get your cat back."*

It was very puzzling, but slowly Lucy and Horace began to understand Finn. They agreed to help her with her game and in return, she told them what they must do to follow Tom Cat.

*"Through a maze made of coral that's the first thing to do.
The route through is tricky, but here is a clue:
look out for clear water, beware of sharp rocks,
watch out for the sharks and avoid any shocks.*

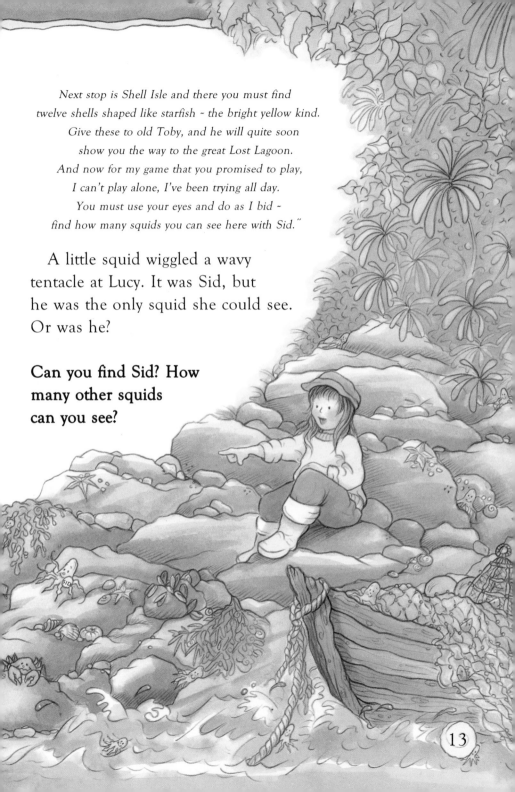

Next stop is Shell Isle and there you must find
twelve shells shaped like starfish - the bright yellow kind.
Give these to old Toby, and he will quite soon
show you the way to the great Lost Lagoon.
And now for my game that you promised to play,
I can't play alone, I've been trying all day.
You must use your eyes and do as I bid -
find how many squids you can see here with Sid."

A little squid wiggled a wavy
tentacle at Lucy. It was Sid, but
he was the only squid she could see.
Or was he?

**Can you find Sid? How
many other squids
can you see?**

13

The Coral Maze

Horace and Lucy said goodbye and set off for the coral maze.

"It's not going to be easy to find a way through," Horace said when they arrived. "The coral is spiky and sharp and there are dangers lurking."

The white flag marks the way out to the open sea. Can you find a way through the maze, steering clear of the spiky coral and lurking creatures?

14

15

Shell Isle

"Phew, I'm glad that's over," said Horace, when they reached the end of the coral maze. "Now let's go to Shell Isle to search for the shells for Toby."

Lucy gasped with astonishment when she saw Shell Isle. Everywhere she looked there were shells gleaming and glittering in the sunshine. There was a shell jetty, a hut made from shells and even a shell boat. The shells looked so pretty that Lucy began to collect them in a basket.

Then she remembered that she had to find some special shells.

Lucy darted up and down. She soon found the twelve yellow star shaped shells and they were ready to look for Toby at the gateway to the Lost Lagoon.

Can you spot the twelve yellow star shells that Lucy needs?

The Lost Lagoon

When Lucy saw Toby she was speechless. He had a fishy tail!

"You're a merman!" she spluttered.

Toby smiled down at her over his glasses. He swished his scaly tail and counted his shells.

"You can go into the Lagoon now," he said.

They sailed on into the Lost Lagoon. At the far side, there were amazing tutti frutti trees growing along the banks.

Just as Lucy and Horace were wondering what to do next, a face popped out of the leaves.

"Hello, I'm Olivia, I study birds," she called. "I get a bird's eye view of the island from up here. I can help you find your furry friend ~ if you help me first. I'm trying to find the Golden Spotted Wonderbird. Its tail has five gold spotted feathers which curl up at the ends. If you can spot it for me, I'll tell you which way your cat went."

Can you spot the Golden Spotted Wonderbird?

The Rainbow River

When Olivia saw the Wonderbird she almost fell out of her tree with excitement.

"Your cat went that way, along the Rainbow River," she pointed.

Lucy stared at the winding, whirling waterway. "It looks a bit choppy," she said.

Horace began to swim.
Waves whipped up as the river
rushed and swirled
hurrying them onward until . . .
Oh no! SPLASH!
SPLUTTER!

Lucy and Horace dived over the edge of a waterfall. Coughing and gasping they bobbed up to the surface again. The Rainbow River roared and raced along to the sea. Suddenly Lucy caught sight of something very familiar.

What has Lucy spotted?

Under the Sea

Tom Cat whizzed around and around in a whirlpool, spinning and sinking down below the waves.

"There's only one way for you to follow him," said Horace, "And luckily help is at hand."

To Lucy's surprise, a small fish began gulping air. With each gulp, the fish puffed up and grew bigger and bigger, until it was enormous.

"It's a puffa fish," Horace told Lucy. "Sit very still."

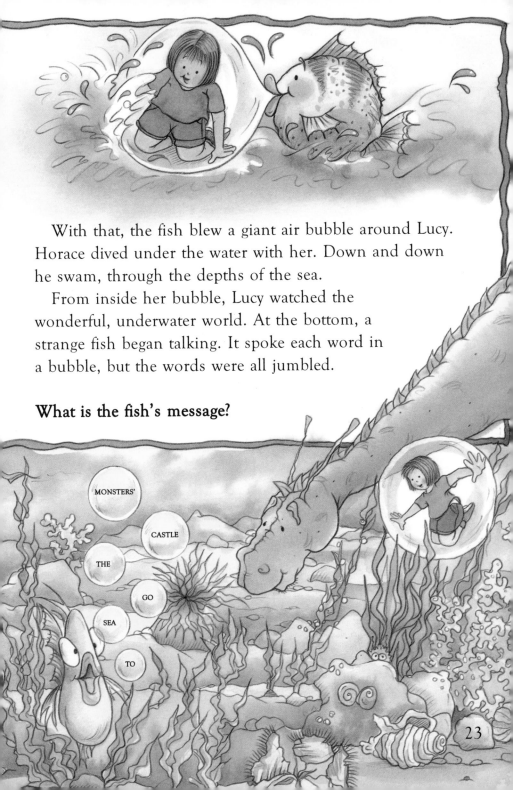

With that, the fish blew a giant air bubble around Lucy.
Horace dived under the water with her. Down and down
he swam, through the depths of the sea.

From inside her bubble, Lucy watched the
wonderful, underwater world. At the bottom, a
strange fish began talking. It spoke each word in
a bubble, but the words were all jumbled.

What is the fish's message?

MONSTERS'

CASTLE

THE

GO

SEA

TO

23

The Galleon

Lucy watched shimmering fish flash past. Two turtles chased each other through coral arches and waving weeds. The reeds rippled apart and Lucy stared ahead into the black mouth of a dark cave and tunnel.

Horace disappeared inside and Lucy followed. The
tunnel ended and Lucy blinked in surprise.
A splendid sunken galleon lay half-buried in the sand.
But Lucy couldn't see Horace anywhere.

Where is Horace? Can you find him?

Horace's Home

"Hold tight," said Horace. "I have a surprise for you."

Lucy clung on to Horace's tail until suddenly she lost her grip. She bounced down and down, tumbling bumpety, bumpety, BUMP. She landed on soft sand and sat staring up at a fantastic fairytale castle.

"It's my home," said Horace. "And here are my family and friends. They all want to meet you but they're a bit shy."

Family? Friends? Lucy could only see fish and funny fishy monsters. But Horace explained that the sea monsters were the ones with two wobbly antennae on their heads.

How many sea monsters do you think there are?

Surprise Party

Lucy followed Horace inside the castle. Her bubble popped and she found she could breathe without it. Horace introduced her to all sorts of sea creatures and led her on to a tall, arched doorway. The gleaming shell doors slowly opened.

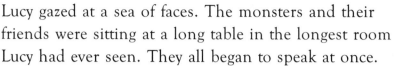

Lucy gazed at a sea of faces. The monsters and their friends were sitting at a long table in the longest room Lucy had ever seen. They all began to speak at once.

"We're having a party to celebrate your visit," said Nessie, Horace's sister. "Our other special guest is already here."

Who is the other special guest?

Goodbye

Lucy gave Tom Cat a big hug and squeeze before she was whisked away to dance. The wonderful party passed in a whirl. Lucy ate and sang and danced . . . until suddenly it was time to go.

Lucy and Tom Cat climbed onto Horace's back and waved goodbye to their new friends. Almost before they knew it, they were back at the beach where their adventure had begun.

"I don't want to say goodbye to you, Horace," Lucy said, hugging him.

Horace smiled, "But I'll see you again very soon."

Lucy and Tom Cat jumped down onto the sandy shore and waved to Horace as he swam back to sea.

"Lucy!" called the familiar voice of her mother. "It's time for supper!"

Answers

Pages 4-5

A green sea monster is coming closer to Lucy's rock. It is circled in the picture.

Pages 6-7

Tom Cat is being washed out to sea.

Pages 8-9

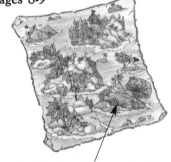

Lucy decides that this must be Blue Bird Island. It is the only one with blue birds on it.

Pages 10-11

This is One Tree Island. It has only one tree, a tower with a pointed turret and there are no other buildings on it.

Pages 12-13

There are eleven little squids including Sid. You can see them all circled here in the picture.

This is Sid the Squid.

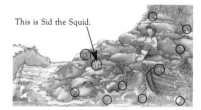

Pages 14-15

Lucy's and Horace's way through the coral maze to the open sea is marked in black.

Pages 16-17

You can see the twelve yellow star shaped shells that Lucy has to find circled here.

Pages 18-19

This is the Golden Spotted Wonderbird. Can you see his five curly tail feathers?

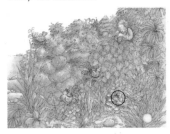

Pages 20-21

Lucy has spotted Tom Cat. Here he is.

Pages 22-23

When you put all the words in the right order, the fish's message is, "GO TO THE SEA MONSTERS' CASTLE."

Pages 24-25

Here is Horace. He is well hidden behind the plants.

Pages 26-27

You can see the ten sea monsters marked here.

Pages 28-29

Did you spot the other special guest? It is Tom Cat.

This edition first published in 2002 by Usborne Publishing Ltd., Usborne House, 83-85 Saffron Hill, London EC1N 8RT, England. www.usborne.com Copyright © 2002, 1995 Usborne Publishing Ltd. The name Usborne and the devices ♀ 🌐 are Trade Marks of Usborne Publishing Ltd. All rights reserved.